The Safari Children's Books
on Good Behavior

Copyright © 2011 Cressida Elias
All rights reserved

Luc the Lion Learns Why it's Important to Brush his Teeth

by
Cressida Elias

Illustrated by Carriel Ann Santos

Luc was a lion who was king of his pride.

The pride was a very large group of lions, lionesses and baby cubs that travelled the African wilderness together.

Now Luc had been the king for more than one year and everyone in his pride loved him.

He was big, strong and had a luxurious, fluffy mane.

He had a huge smile that showed off his sharp, sparkling teeth that other lions admired greatly.

But more importantly, he was a good king.

He led his pride to water when they were thirsty, to food when they were hungry ...

and to shade when they needed rest.

Before he was king, he had to learn how to be a leader and at the same time, be part of a team.

But these lessons were not easy for Luc.

He had to learn to run fast,

...share his food

...exercise his muscles,

...roar loudly,

...protect the young cubs...

and last of all, brush his teeth.

Luc's Dad taught him that if he brushed his teeth everyday, he would have the best teeth in the pride and they would sparkle in the sunshine...

...just like his.

But Luc didn't like brushing his teeth. It was boring and he wanted to be out in the wilderness learning how to hunt.

He thought that was much more important!

One day, during Luc's Kingly lessons, his Dad reminded him to brush his teeth again.

Luc sighed and thought of how he should be hunting and chasing other animals.

He asked his Dad,

'Why do I need my teeth to sparkle?'

'Because if they sparkle, son,' said his Dad, 'it means they are healthy and strong and you will be able to eat good food.

If you eat good food, your body will be healthy and strong...and you will stay king for many, many years.'

'It will also set a good example to everyone else in the pride that brushing your teeth is important for your health and your looks'.

Luc's Dad roared.

Yes, his teeth were very impressive thought Luc, and very scary too.

His breath was sweet as well, not stale like some lions.

Luc roared and looked at his own teeth in the mirror.

Oh, what a disappointment, they were yellow and had his breakfast all over them.

He got out his toothbrush and gave them a good brush.

He looked again and this time his teeth sparkled.

'Phew!' he thought, 'it's not too late to start looking after my teeth so they stay strong.'

So Luc began to clean his teeth every day.

'My teeth are going to be great, just like me!', he thought...

...and they were!

The End

Safari Children's Books on Good Behavior

other books:

Gerry the Giraffe Learns why it's Good to Share

Bonbon the Butterfly Learns Why it's Important to Think of Others and not just Herself

Ellena the elephant Learns Why she Needs to Tidy up Her Toys

Maxi the Monkey Learns why Going to Bed Early is Important

Printed in Great Britain
by Amazon